ADVENTURES AT CAMP LOTS-O-FUN

MARILYN HELMER

ILLUSTRATED BY MIKE DEAS

D1007371

ORCA BOOK PUBLISHERS

To Cameron, Riley and Andrew,
three very adventurous guys. —M.H.

Text copyright © 2010 Marilyn Helmer
Illustrations copyright © 2010 Mike Deas

Library and Archives Canada Cataloguing in Publication

Helmer, Marilyn
Adventures at Camp Lots-o-fun / written by Marilyn Helmer ; illustrated
by Mike Deas.
(Orca echoes)

Also available in an electronic format.
ISBN 978-1-55469-347-4

I. Deas, Mike, 1982- II. Title. III. Series: Orca echoes.
PS8565.E4594A73 2010   jc813'.54   C2010-903523-2

First published in the United States, 2010
Library of Congress Control Number: 2010928734

Summary: DJ's wild imagination takes the boys in Cabin Six by surprise
and makes for an adventurous, fun-filled week at summer camp.

Orca Book Publishers gratefully acknowledges the support for its publishing programs
provided by the following agencies: the Government of Canada through the Canada Book Fund
and the Canada Council for the Arts, and the Province of British Columbia
through the BC Arts Council and the Book Publishing Tax Credit.

Mixed Sources
Cert no. SW-COC-001271
© 1996 FSC
FSC

*Orca Book Publishers is dedicated to preserving the environment and has printed this book
on paper certified by the Forest Stewardship Council.*

Typesetting by Teresa Bubela
Cover artwork and interior illustrations by Mike Deas
Author photo by Gary Helmer

ORCA BOOK PUBLISHERS   ORCA BOOK PUBLISHERS
PO BOX 5626, STN. B   PO BOX 468
VICTORIA, BC CANADA   CUSTER, WA USA
V8R 6S4   98240-0468

www.orcabook.com
Printed and bound in Canada.

13 12 11 10 • 4 3 2 1

CHAPTER ONE
CAMP NOT-SO-FUN

DJ sat on the bottom bunk, chewing the end of his pencil. He read over what he had written.

Dear Lots-o-Fun Journal,

Here I am at Camp Lots-o-Fun. Me and the other guys in Cabin Six call it Camp Not-so-Fun. It's on Great Bear Lake. But we can't go swimming or canoeing or any of that fun stuff. It's been raining since we got here. Some of the puddles are so big there are creepy crawlers in them. There are bugs and mosquitoes all over the place!

Chris sprayed our cabin with Bug-Be-Gone. He's our counselor. His hair is so long he wears it in a ponytail.

He has big muscles too. He showed us his biceps. They look like boulders. You don't want to mess with Chris. I hope the Bug-Be-Gone works. I saw a cockroach in the dining hall this morning. Raj said it was a cricket, but he didn't have his glasses on. I know a cockroach when I see one.

Buggily yours,
DJ

DJ looked at the other boys in Cabin Six. Raj, Ernie and Andrew were sprawled on the floor, making their journals. DJ had finished his yesterday. He had also made a monkey mask, a bucket hat and a rock paperweight. He was tired of crafts.

DJ glanced at the rain-streaked window. Wait a minute. Something yellow peeked through the trees. DJ shot to his feet. "The sun's out!" he shouted.

Chris opened the door. "Looks like it's clearing up. Get your rain gear, guys. We're going for a hike."

The boys scrambled for their jackets and boots. DJ rummaged through his duffel bag. His fingers touched something soft. He started to pull it out. When he realized it wasn't his rain jacket, he shoved it back into his bag.

"DJ, hurry up. We're waiting to go," said Andrew. He swiped his dark hair off his forehead.

"I'm looking for my rain jacket," said DJ. He remembered taking the jacket out of his bag to pack something else. Something he had decided to bring at the last minute. But had he remembered to put his jacket back in?

"You did bring a jacket, right?" Chris asked.

"I think I forgot it," said DJ.

"There's a Lost and Found in the dining hall," said Chris. "See if you can find something there."

The Lost and Found was crammed full. DJ found a jacket among the jumble and pulled it out.

The jacket was bright green. Across the front, in big letters, were the words *Girl Power*. DJ groaned. He couldn't wear that jacket. The guys would laugh at him.

DJ stared at the letters. He dashed to the supply cupboard and grabbed a roll of red tape. He taped over the word *Girl*. Then he taped the word *Man* after *Power*.

"Did you find something?" Chris asked through the screen door.

"Yup," DJ shouted back. He shrugged into the jacket and ran outside. "Meet—Power Man!" he said, pumping his fists in the air.

The hike was fun, even if the woods were wet.

DJ led the way. His red hair was curlier than usual from the dampness. It stuck out the sides of his baseball cap. DJ didn't care. He liked his hair the way it was.

Thoughts raced through DJ's mind. He could climb the tallest tree. He could leap over the biggest rock. Power Man wasn't afraid of anything.

DJ spotted an empty bird's nest, high in an old dead tree. "Power Man can climb up and get it," he said.

"No way," said Chris. "I want Power Man on the ground where I can keep an eye on him."

6

DJ sighed. What was the fun of being Power Man if he couldn't do any power stuff?

The boys stopped to rest in a grassy clearing. Chris passed out juice boxes and granola bars.

Andrew sat across from DJ, gobbling down his granola bar. DJ thought Andrew had the biggest teeth he had ever seen. No wonder he could eat so fast.

"Let's play I Spy," said Andrew, brushing crumbs from his mouth. "I'll go first. I spy something that begins with the letter *B*."

Everyone took turns guessing. "Nope," Andrew said each time. "It's your turn, DJ. I bet you won't guess it either."

DJ wasn't listening. He stared into the woods. Something was moving among the trees. Something very big. Something very hairy. Something very, very scary.

"Bear!" shouted DJ.

Andrew snickered. "Dumb guess. I don't see any bears around here."

DJ pointed to the trees. "Then what's that?"

Four pairs of eyes followed DJ's finger. Something *was* moving among the trees. Something very big. Something very hairy. Something very, very scary.

DJ shot to his feet. "It's a bear. Run for your life!"

The boys took off in a screaming, screeching scramble. "Wait! Stop! Come back!" Chris shouted after them. "There are no bears around here."

Nobody waited. Nobody stopped. Nobody came back. The boys from Cabin Six raced toward Camp Lots-o-Fun as fast as their legs could carry them.

The boys burst through the trees at the end of the path.

Another group of campers was heading out for a hike.

"Run! Run! There's a humongous bear chasing us," DJ said as they raced past the startled group.

When they reached the cabin, DJ slammed the door behind them. "We're safe," he gasped. "That old bear can't get us in here."

"Hold on." Ernie's voice squeaked. His short spiky blond hair stood up like a bristle brush. "Where is Chris?"

Suddenly the door flew open. Chris staggered in. His jacket was torn. His jeans were muddy. His face was streaked with dirt.

Raj's eyes widened. "Did you get in a fight with the bear?"

"No, I did not." Chris stopped to catch his breath. "There was no bear. It was only a big dog."

"But I saw it," said DJ. "It was humongous. Like fifty feet tall. It had claws like daggers and huge hungry teeth."

Chris sank into a chair. "What you saw, DJ, was a big dog. A. Big. Dog." He said each word slowly. It reminded DJ of the way his mom spoke to him when she was cross.

"How did you get so dirty?" asked Andrew.

"I fell," said Chris. "Twice." He stood up. "It's lunchtime. I want you all to go straight to the dining hall. I'm going to get cleaned up."

The dining hall was in chaos. Everyone was talking at once.

"Did you hear? A kid got eaten by a bear."

"Some kids were chased by a whole pack of bears."

"The bear was huge."

"I want to go home!"

Mike, the head counselor, stood at the front of the room. He blew his whistle—*Blast! Blast! Blast!*

"Listen up, everyone." Mike's voice boomed. "There is no bear. There are no bears anywhere near here." He glared around the room. "If I hear one more bear story, there's going to be trouble with a capital *T*."

"But…" DJ stood up.

Andrew grabbed his arm. "Be quiet," he hissed. "You'll get us all in trouble."

DJ sat down again. They would be in a lot more trouble if that bear had followed them back to Camp Lots-o-Fun.

CHAPTER FOUR
SOCKSTER

Dear Lots-o-Fun Journal,

No rain today. We haven't seen the bear again. Maybe he got lost in the woods.

We went swimming this morning. Chris said we should swim out to the raft. I told him that wasn't a good idea. There are horrible things on the bottom of the lake. They look like weeds, but they aren't. They are monsters with wavy tentacles.

I saw one of the monsters gobble up a giant fish. It swam into a big clump of tentacles. But it didn't swim out the other side! When I told Chris about the monsters, he rolled his eyes. He does that a lot. He's going to be sorry if campers start disappearing.

This afternoon we made pinecone crafts. Chris told us pine trees grow from pinecones. I had a fan-tabulous idea! I collected a whole bunch of pinecones. I'm going to plant them in our garden. Mom and Dad will be so surprised when they find a pine forest in our backyard.

Dinnertime. Got to go.

Hungrily yours,
DJ, a.k.a. Power Man!

At the group campfire that evening, there was a sing-along. DJ loved to sing. He sang louder than anyone else.

The rosy sunset faded into darkness. Faces glowed in the flickering firelight. Night closed in around them. Finally, Mike said, "It's time for one last song."

DJ sprang to his feet. "Can we sing 'Row, Row, Row Your Boat'? I made up a new verse. *Row, row, row your boat, gently down the stream. There's a bear* out in the woods and that will make us scream," he sang.

Some of the campers laughed. Others glanced nervously at the woods.

At lights-out, the boys returned to their cabin. DJ woke up in the middle of the night. The cabin was pitch-black. He heard a humongous splash coming from the lake. Then another. What was out there?

DJ scrambled out of bed. He rummaged through his duffel bag. His fingers touched something soft. He pulled it out and climbed back into bed.

DJ wrapped his arm around his sock monkey. "Don't be scared, Sockster," he whispered. "Power Man will keep you safe."

The next morning, before anyone else was awake, DJ tucked Sockster back into his duffel bag.

"Does everyone have his life jacket on?" asked Chris.

"Yes," the boys answered.

"Okay. Two in a canoe. Andrew and Raj in one. DJ and Ernie in the other," said Chris. "I'll bring up the rear."

DJ climbed into the closest canoe. "You know what, Ernie?" he said. "Last night I heard a humongous splash. I'll bet it was that giant fish. Maybe it wasn't eaten by the lake monsters after all."

Ernie hesitated. "I think I'll stay on the dock."

"Ernie, hurry up and get into the canoe," Chris said. "We're ready to go."

"Don't worry, Ernie," said DJ. "I'll protect you. If a big old giant fish attacks us, Power Man will give him a karate chop."

The boys paddled along the shore until they came to a small bay. The lake's surface was as smooth as a mirror. DJ looked over the side. "I see the giant fish!" he shouted.

Ernie screeched. A pair of startled fishermen glared at them from their boat.

Chris paddled alongside their canoe. "What's going on?" he asked DJ.

"There's a giant fish down there." DJ pointed. "I think it's following us."

Ernie clutched the side of the canoe. "I want to go back to camp," he said.

Chris stared into the water. "Calm down, Ernie. It's just an old log."

Andrew and Raj paddled over. "I see it," said Raj, pushing his glasses up on his nose. "I think it's moving."

"The ripples from your paddle make it look like it's moving around," said Chris. "Come on, it's time to head back."

Andrew looked at DJ. "Only sissies believe in monsters and giant fish," he scoffed.

DJ didn't answer. He stared into the water. Something was down there all right. Something that moved. Something that looked like a giant fish. DJ swallowed but he wasn't scared. Power Man would never be scared.

"Let's go, DJ," said Ernie, snatching up his paddle.

DJ grabbed his own paddle. They were the first ones back to the dock.

That night DJ slept with Sockster again. Just in case Sockster was scared.

CHAPTER SIX
A SURPRISE

Cabin Six was in an uproar. Chris had announced they were going on an overnight camping trip. "After breakfast tomorrow morning, we're off to Hermit Island," he said.

"Does a real hermit live there?" asked DJ.

Chris shook his head. "The island is deserted. But it's a cool place to camp."

Deserted? DJ's thoughts took off like a racehorse. "Maybe it isn't deserted," he said. "Maybe it's haunted by the hermit's ghost."

Chris rolled his eyes. "Hermit Island is not haunted," he said.

"Besides, there's no such thing as ghosts," said Andrew.

DJ stood his ground. "What about Halloween?"

"They are only pretend ghosts," Andrew said.

"I read a book about a ghost," said Raj. "It was a true story. The ghost lived in a big old haunted house."

Chris's hand shot up like a Stop sign. "There is no hermit on Hermit Island. There are no ghosts on Hermit Island. There is nothing on Hermit Island but rocks and trees."

"But maybe…," DJ said.

Chris raised his hand again. "It's bedtime," he said. "Let's get a good night's sleep."

DJ went to bed. But he did not go to sleep. His mind whirled. What if the hermit's ghost was guarding Hermit Island? What if the ghost did not like visitors?

Once again, DJ slipped out of bed. He rummaged through his duffel bag. Power Man might not be scared. But that didn't mean Sockster wasn't.

"This place is awesome," said Raj as they pulled the canoes up onto the beach.

"Grab your gear and follow me," said Chris. "We'll get our tent set up. Then we'll go exploring."

Ahead was a grassy clearing surrounded by towering spruce and pine trees. DJ wished he could go exploring right away. But an hour later, they were still struggling to set up the tent. It had already collapsed three times.

"Don't worry, Chris," said DJ. "If we can't get the tent up, we can rough it."

"What's roughing it?" asked Ernie.

"We can sleep outside," said DJ. "It's really fun. You can see the stars and everything."

"Are there snakes around here?" asked Raj.

"I'm not sleeping outside," said Ernie.

Chris stood up. "The tent is all set now. Let's go for a hike."

"Are we going into the woods?" asked Ernie. "What if we get lost again?" His eyes darted toward the trees. "What if that bear swam over here?"

"Don't worry, Ernie," said DJ. "Bears can't swim."

Andrew folded his arms across his chest. "Yes, they can," he said. "Bears can swim anywhere."

Ernie shivered. "I'm not going into the woods."

Chris raised both hands. "I don't want to hear another word about bears," he said. "There are no bears on Hermit Island. Follow me, guys. We'll walk along the beach."

DJ followed the others, practicing his karate chops, just in case.

CHAPTER EIGHT
NOISES IN THE NIGHT

DJ picked up a stick and wrote *Power Man Was Here* in the wet sand. That would scare away any old ghost.

As he ran to catch up with the others, he spotted something caught under a rock. "Hey, guys, look what I found," he said, holding it up.

"E-e-e-w!" Andrew made a gagging sound. "It's a yucky old shoe."

"Maybe it belongs to the hermit," said DJ. "Maybe he's looking for it."

Chris sighed. "Bring it back to camp, DJ. We'll put it in the garbage."

Later, Chris showed the boys how to build a campfire. They roasted hotdogs for dinner and toasted marshmallows for dessert.

The night grew dark and still. The moon was as pale as milk. A breeze blew across the lake. The trees swayed as if they were dancing.

"Let's tell ghost stories," said DJ. "I know a good one. It's really scary. L-o-o-ong ago, on a d-a-a-ark, stormy night like this one—," he began in a spooky voice.

"It's not stormy tonight," Andrew said.

Raj nudged Andrew. "Be quiet. I want to hear the story."

"Some campers heard a cre-e-e-eping, sne-e-e-aking sound," DJ whispered. He loved scary stories. "They were alone on a deserted island. Suddenly a horrible thing sprang from the darkness. It was the hermit's ghost!"

Ernie moved closer to DJ.

"Their tent had blown away in the storm." DJ's voice rose. "They had nowhere to hide. But one of

the campers was really brave. He knew how to do karate." DJ whirled his arms around like a windmill. "He saved everyone because he was—Power Man!"

"Awesome story," said Raj.

"It was boring," said Andrew. "It wasn't even scary."

"It was so scary," Ernie said. "I have goose bumps all over my arms."

Andrew shrugged. "No dumb ghost story scares me."

"Enough, Andrew," said Chris. "It's time for bed. Let's go, guys."

Late that night, DJ woke up. He heard a creeping, sneaking sound. He felt around in the bottom of his sleeping bag. Then he searched his backpack. Where was Sockster? DJ's heart sank. Sockster was back at Camp Lots-o-Fun, hidden under his pillow.

DJ heard the creeping sound again. He froze. Wait a minute. He was Power Man. Power Man couldn't be scared. DJ reached for his flashlight. He unzipped the tent flap and tiptoed outside.

The pale moon cast long shadows through the trees. Suddenly a ghostly sound echoed through the silence. "Whoo-hoo-oo! Whoo-hoo-oo!"

A hand grabbed DJ's shoulder. DJ screeched. "Help! Help! The hermit's ghost has got me!"

Chris's voice rumbled in his ear. "DJ, what are you doing out here?"

DJ sighed with relief. "I heard a creeping, sneaking sound." He gulped. "It must be the hermit's ghost. He's coming to get his shoe."

Chris let out a groan. "There is no such thing as a ghost, DJ." He jerked a thumb over his shoulder. "Get back into the tent and go to sleep."

"But...," DJ said.

Chris pointed at DJ. Then he pointed to the tent.

DJ scrambled inside. He slid into his sleeping bag. Why hadn't he brought Sockster? Sockster was back at Camp Lots-o-Fun, all alone. And he was probably scared. Really, really scared.

Dear Lots-o-Fun Journal,

We're back at camp now. That old hermit's ghost didn't get us. I'll bet my karate chops scared him off.

Remember the pinecones I was saving? Chris found them under my bed. They smelled kind of funky. Chris said they were full of bugs. He made me throw them away. So no pine forest for me.

We went blueberry picking. We got lots of deerfly bites. We hardly found any blueberries. I think that bear got to them first. We're going to eat the blueberries for a snack. Maybe with ice cream. Yummers!

Buggily yours,
DJ, a.k.a. Power Man!

That afternoon the boys went swimming and played beach volleyball. They came back to the cabin to change before dinner.

"Listen up, guys," said Chris. "Ernie's not feeling well. I'm going to take him to the nurse. I'll be back in a few minutes." He looked around the cabin. "No nonsense while I'm gone."

The minute Chris and Ernie left, Raj grabbed his pillow. He whacked Andrew. Andrew grabbed his pillow and whacked Raj. Laughter exploded through the cabin.

DJ snatched up his pillow to join in the fight. A gray blur flew across the room. DJ watched in horror as Sockster landed at Andrew's feet.

Andrew picked up Sockster. "Whose dolly is this?" he asked, dangling Sockster by his tail.

DJ stepped forward. "He's mine. And he's not a dolly. He's a sock monkey."

Andrew let out a snort of laughter. "Hey, Raj, let's have a monkey fight." He ducked around DJ and threw Sockster to Raj.

Raj caught Sockster and threw him back to Andrew. Back and forth Sockster flew as DJ tried to rescue him.

Sockster landed in Andrew's hands. "If you want your dolly, go get him," said Andrew. He whipped Sockster toward the doorway.

At that moment, Chris walked in the door. Sockster hit him in the face and fell to the floor.

The boys froze.

Chris snatched up Sockster. "Who does this belong to?" he asked in a voice like rumbling thunder.

DJ swallowed. "He's mine," he said.

Chris handed Sockster to DJ. "Does anyone care to tell me what's been going on here?" he asked.

Silence. Finally DJ spoke. "We were having a pillow fight," he said.

Chris glared. "Did you start it?" he asked.

"We all did," said Raj.

"Get those pillows back on your beds," Chris said. "It's almost dinnertime."

DJ turned to his bunk. As he put Sockster into his duffel bag, Andrew smirked. DJ pretended not to notice.

The next afternoon, the boys were in their cabin changing out of their swim trunks.

"DJ," Andrew hissed, poking his head through the neck of his T-shirt. "Where's your dolly?"

DJ clenched his jaw. He felt deep-down sad. He didn't feel like Power Man anymore. He almost wished he hadn't brought Sockster.

Chris's voice cut into his thoughts. "Gather around, guys. We're going to look at stars."

"How can we look at stars now?" asked Ernie. "It's still daylight."

Chris took a book from his duffel bag. "We're going to read up on stars. I also brought a DVD

37

about constellations. We'll watch it in the dining hall after dinner. Tonight we can do some serious stargazing."

"Awesome," said Raj.

DJ forgot his woes. "My dad has a telescope," he said. "He showed me a whole bunch of constellations."

"I know everything about constellations," said Andrew. "They're groups of stars that have names."

"Everyone knows that," said Raj. "Hey, maybe we can find a new constellation."

"Fan-tabulous!" said DJ. "And we can name it too."

"You don't know anything," said Andrew. "You have to be an astronomer to find a new constellation."

DJ didn't hear him. Scurrying across the floor was the biggest, creepiest spider he had ever seen.

"A humongous spider ran under your bed, Andrew. I think it's a tarantula!" said DJ.

Andrew jumped onto his bunk. He looked as if his eyes were about to pop out of his head. "Get it out of here. I hate spiders!"

"Calm down, Andrew," said Chris. He frowned at DJ. "There are no tarantulas around here."

DJ shook his head. "It was humongous. It had fat legs and fangs like a tarantula."

Chris looked under Andrew's bed. "There's nothing but dust under here."

"But I saw it," said DJ.

Andrew turned to DJ. "That was a dumb trick. You can't fool me. There are no huge spiders in here."

Raj grinned at Andrew. "You sure were scared when you thought there was one," he said.

Andrew glared at DJ. "I'm not afraid of anything."

DJ glared back. "I saw a humongous spider. And it crawled right under your bed."

"Forget it, DJ," said Andrew. "You're not going to get me to fall for a dumb trick like that."

As soon as it was dark, Chris and the boys went down to the dock.

"There must be a million stars in the sky," Ernie said, looking up.

"There's Ursa Major." Andrew pointed. "It's the Great Bear. And see those seven stars?"

"That's the Big Dipper," said DJ.

Raj looked. "Where?"

"There. See? It looks like a pot with a long handle," said DJ.

Raj followed DJ's finger. "Awesome," he said.

"Watch," said Chris. He drew a line with his finger through the bowl in the Big Dipper.

41

"There's the North Star. Does anyone know another name for it?"

"Polaris," DJ and Andrew answered together.

Andrew pointed. "Over there is Cassiopeia."

"I just saw a falling star," said DJ.

Ernie stared at the sky. "I can't see it."

"It's gone now," said DJ. "It must have fallen all the way to the ground."

Andrew made a snorting sound. "Stars don't fall to the ground."

"They might," said DJ.

"They don't," Andrew said.

"Hey, guys, look!" Raj pointed. "Those stars look like a dinosaur."

"You're dreaming," said Andrew.

"They do look like a dinosaur," said DJ. "Like a Tyrannosaurus rex. Hey, maybe we have discovered a new constellation."

"It doesn't look like any dinosaur I've ever seen," said Andrew.

42

"How many dinosaurs have you seen?" asked DJ.

A shout came from a nearby cabin. "Quiet out there. We're trying to sleep!"

"It's late," said Chris. "Enough stargazing for tonight."

Back in Cabin Six, everyone fell asleep quickly. But they didn't sleep for long. The still night was shattered by a scream of terror: "Help! There's a huge spider crawling up my arm."

CHAPTER TWELVE
POWER MAN TO THE RESCUE

Chris flicked the lights on.

Andrew hopped around the room. His eyes were wide with fright. "Where is it? It was crawling up my arm!" he shouted.

"There it goes." Raj pointed. A large spider scurried across the floor.

Ernie huddled in the top bunk. "I see it!" he said.

"I told you I saw a tarantula," said DJ.

The boys went wild, screeching and shouting, "Tarantula! Tarantula!"

Chris rolled his eyes. "It's not a tarantula."

No one was listening.

Lights went on in other cabins. Mike appeared in their doorway. "What is going on here?" He glared at everyone. "You're waking up the whole camp."

"There's a tarantula in our cabin," said DJ.

Mike looked around the room. "I don't see any spiders," he said.

The spider had disappeared. Panic broke out again. Not seeing the spider was almost as scary as seeing it.

"Spiders like darkness," said Mike. He grabbed a flashlight and looked under the beds. "There it goes." He whistled. "It is a big one. But it's just a harmless fishing spider. It won't hurt you." He wiggled the bed and the spider scurried out.

"Step on it! Squash it!" Andrew shouted.

DJ gasped. Kill it? No way. This was a job for Power Man.

DJ spotted the blueberry bowl. He grabbed it and clamped it over the spider. Blueberries rolled across the floor like marbles.

Andrew screamed. "Don't let it get away."

With a quick swoop, DJ flipped the bowl upright. The spider sat safely on the bottom.

"Good work, DJ," said Mike.

Raj clapped DJ on the back. "You are so brave."

DJ grinned. "Power Man has to be brave." He turned to Andrew. "My mom's scared of spiders too. I catch them for her all the time."

Andrew shuddered. "Get it out of here."

DJ looked in the bowl. The spider's legs were long, but they weren't fat, and it didn't have any fangs.

"It looked a lot bigger on the floor," said Raj.

"And a lot scarier," said Ernie.

"It's the one who looks scared now," said DJ.

Mike reached for the bowl. "I'll turn it loose outside."

After Mike left, they cleaned up the spilled blueberries. "We forgot to have our snack tonight," said Chris.

"Lucky we had the bowl," said DJ. "Otherwise Power Man might have had to catch the spider with his bare hands."

Ernie peered down from the top bunk. "Would you really pick it up with your hands?"

"That would be a dumb thing to do," said Andrew.

Chris swung around. He put a hand on Andrew's shoulder. "I do not want to hear the word *dumb* coming from your mouth again," he said. "Is that clear?"

Andrew's face went fire-engine red. He stared at the floor. "Sorry," he muttered.

"Back to bed, guys," said Chris. "Let's try to get some sleep."

DJ didn't go to sleep right away. Thoughts scurried through his head. Wouldn't a spider make a great pet for Power Man? DJ sat up, almost bumping his head on the top bunk. Maybe I can ask all my friends to give me one for my birthday. Maybe I can have a whole family of spiders! Fan-tabulous!

Dear Lots-o-Fun Journal,

Whew, no more spider attacks last night. It was raining when we got up this morning. So I had to wear my Power Man jacket. And guess what? At breakfast, everyone was talking about the tarantula I caught last night. Mike told them it wasn't a tarantula. It was just a fishing spider. No one believed him.

Today is our last day at Camp Lots-o-Fun. We're all going home tomorrow. Today is Lots-o-Fun Day. We've had races and games and a whole bunch of fun stuff. Guess what else? Cabin Six got the most points. We each got a Camp Lots-o-Fun T-shirt. Fan-tabulous!

We're supposed to be resting now. I told Chris that

Power Man never needs to rest. Chris told me sometimes
he needs a rest from Power Man. I think that was a
joke. Chris has a weird sense of humor sometimes.

I think everyone has rested by now. Got to go—it's
time for our nature scavenger hunt.

Scavengely yours,
DJ, a.k.a. Power Man!

Chris handed Raj and DJ each a piece of paper.
"This is a list of the things you have to find," he
said. "You'll work in pairs. Raj, you work with Ernie.
DJ, you work with Andrew."

DJ and Andrew stared at each other. Andrew
frowned. DJ frowned too. Before either of them
could protest, Chris gave them their instructions.

"This is a nature scavenger hunt," Chris said.
"Only things you find in nature count." He grinned.
"Get busy, guys, and good luck."

DJ read the list again. "Something old, something new, something yellow, something blue. Something rough, something round, something lost, something found."

"So far we have a rock for old and a mushroom for round," said Andrew.

"And a pinecone for rough," DJ added. Moments later, he picked up a twig. It was covered with tiny buds. "Here's our new," he said.

Andrew shrugged. "What's new about a twig?"

"The buds are new leaves," said DJ.

"Oh, yeah, okay," said Andrew.

Raj and Ernie ran past. "We've already found five things," Raj shouted over his shoulder.

"Bet that's more than you guys have."

"Not for long," Andrew shouted back. He turned to DJ. "I know what we can use for yellow," he said. "Follow me."

Andrew led the way to the back of the cabin. A clump of bright yellow buttercups glowed like sunshine. Andrew picked one.

DJ saw something out of the corner of his eye. It was a gray, black and white feather. He picked it up and stuck it in his cap.

"We need something blue," said Andrew.

DJ thought for a moment. "Blueberries! Remember the blueberries I spilled when I caught the spider? We cleaned them up, but maybe we missed one."

They raced into the cabin and started searching.

"I see one," said Andrew.

DJ spun around. As he did, his foot came down, smack on top of the blueberry. "Oh, no," he groaned.

"Maybe it's stuck to the bottom of your shoe," said Andrew.

DJ yanked off his shoe. On the bottom was a blue blob. He showed it to Andrew. "All we've got is a blobby blue blueblerry," he said.

Andrew looked at DJ and burst out laughing. "No, we've got a bobby blue booblerry," he said.

DJ clutched his stomach. "Or a blobbily blue booblerry." He and Andrew collapsed in a giggling, snorting heap.

Outside, Chris's whistle shrilled. "Time's up," he called.

DJ scrambled to his feet. "We haven't got a lost yet, or a found."

Andrew frowned. "Wait a minute." He pointed to DJ's cap. "Your feather can be our found."

"But we still don't have a lost," said DJ.

Chris came into the cabin. Raj and Ernie were right behind him. "Did you find everything on the list?" asked Raj.

"We found everything except round," said Ernie.

"We found everything except lost," said Andrew.

"Let's have a look," said Chris.

Raj held their bag open.

Ernie pulled out a smelly pinecone for old and a seedpod for new. For yellow and blue they had a mushroom with a yellow cap and half a robin's eggshell.

"What do you have for rough, lost and found?" asked Chris.

Raj produced a piece of bark for rough and a snail shell for found. "And look what we have for lost," he said. He held up a slim brown object. "A porcupine quill."

"That's not a porcupine quill," said Andrew. "It's a pine needle."

"I told you it was a pine needle," said Ernie.

"It still counts," said Raj. "The pine tree lost one of its needles." He looked at Andrew. "Let's see what you found."

Andrew and DJ spread out their finds.

"I don't think we should count the squashed blueberry," said Raj. "You found it indoors."

"Squashed or not, it's still blue," said Chris. "And blueberries grow in nature."

"You still didn't find everything on your list," said Ernie. "So no one won."

While everyone was talking, DJ was using his Power-Man thinking. "We did win!" he said. He snatched up the feather. "This is our found *and* our lost," he declared. "A bird lost the feather before we found it."

"No fair," said Raj. "You can't use one thing for both."

"I think it is fair," said Chris. "I didn't say you couldn't use the same item twice." He turned to DJ and Andrew. "Congratulations, guys. You two make a good team."

DJ and Andrew grinned and gave each other a high five.

CHAPTER FIFTEEN
GOING HOME

After breakfast the next morning, everyone packed up to go home. DJ put Sockster into his backpack extra carefully. He checked twice to be sure Sockster was safe.

Soon the buses were loaded. Chris sat beside DJ. He put his seat back and closed his eyes.

DJ pulled his journal out of his backpack.

Dear Lots-o-Fun Journal,

We're ready to go home. We're just waiting for the bus driver.

Camp Lots-o-Fun was LOTS OF FUN. I feel sad saying goodbye to Chris and the guys in my cabin.

But guess what? They're all coming back next summer. And we are all going to ask if we can be in the same cabin again. Even Andrew. He's really nice when you get to know him. And guess what else—I got the award for the Most Fun Camper. I voted for me, and so did everyone else.

I got a postcard from my mom a couple of days ago. She said things are really quiet when I'm not around. I'll bet they have all been really bored. But they'll start having fun again when I get home.

That's all the news for now. Wait a minute. The driver just got on the bus. He looks kind of weird. He has big silver eyes. He has a pointy head.

I don't think this is a bus at all. I think it's a spaceship. We're about to blast off. Goodbye, Camp Lots-o-Fun! We're on our way to the moon!

Alienly yours,
DJ, a.k.a Power Man!

MARILYN HELMER is the author of many children's books, including picturebooks, early readers, novels, riddle books and retold tales. Marilyn says one of the best sources for story ideas is her own children. With imagination and a dab of exaggeration, she turns their exploits and adventures into stories other children enjoy reading.

Adventures at Camp Lots-o-Fun is Marilyn's fourth book with Orca. *Dinosaurs on the Beach*, an Orca Young Reader, was published in 2003. *Sharing Snowy* (2008) and *The Fossil Hunters* (2009) are both part of the Orca Echoes series. Marilyn and her husband Gary live in Belwood near Fergus, Ontario.